It was a bitter...
Christmas was the b...

Old man Scrooge was counting his precious gold when his clerk, Bob Cratchit, interrupted. "Mr. Forbes was collecting for the orphanage, sir. He hoped you could spare some change."

"What! Give my money away? Never! Let some other fool buy clothes for those children. As for you, Cratchit, worry about your own family and be thankful you have a job."

Cratchit quickly grabbed his coat and headed for the door. "Yes, sir, yes, sir. Merry Christmas, sir."

"Christmas. Humph," muttered Scrooge.

When the door opened again, he scowled. "What is it now? Can't I have any peace!"

"It's me Marian, Uncle. I've brought a lovely wreath to cheer you up."

"Well, take it back. I won't hang the silly thing."

"Don't be so grumpy. I'm inviting you to dinner tomorrow. You're my only family, and it would mean so much."

"Nonsense! My father didn't believe in Christmas and neither do I. Now leave me alone, Marian. I'm a busy man." Saddened by her uncle's rejection, Marian left the shop.

Scrooge shivered. He glanced out the window and saw that it was snowing again. Soon the drifts would make it impossible to walk. Reluctantly he put away his gold and headed home.

The blustery wind pushed him along and the snow stung his eyes.

Moments later, Scrooge was sitting by the fire. He sighed, "Whew. Home at last. No one would dare bother me here."

Suddenly, a loud clanking noise made him bolt from his chair. "Who's there? Answer me, at once!"

Someone moaned in terrible pain. In the middle of the room, not three feet from Scrooge's chair, stood the ghost of his long dead partner, Joseph Marley!

"Listen to me, Ebeneezer Scrooge: Unless you change your wicked ways, you, too, will be doomed to wear chains and walk this earth forever. Before this night is over, you will be visited by three spirits. Look carefully at what they show you, and learn your lesson well. For this is your last chance." With a final clank of his chains, Marley vanished.

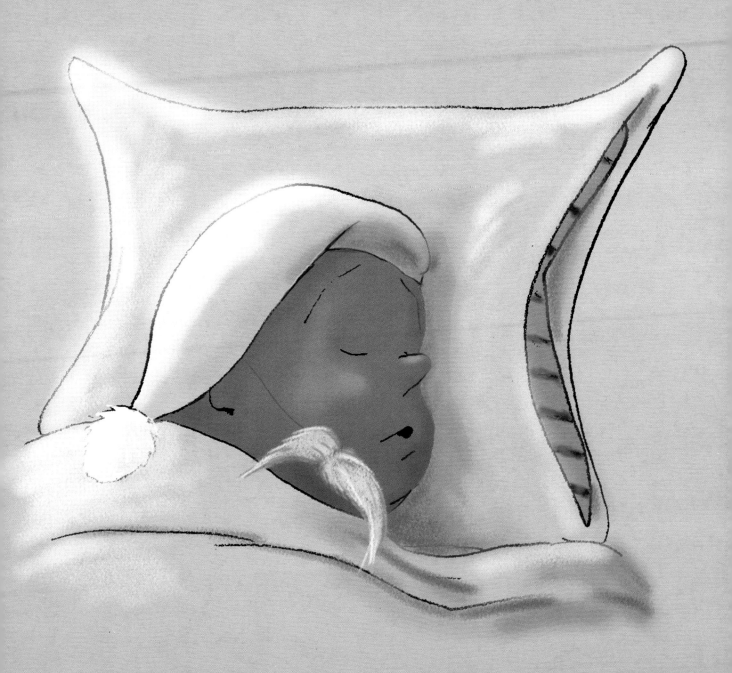

"I'm so tired. I must be seeing things," Scrooge said. As soon as his head hit the pillow, he was asleep. But not for long. When the clock on the mantel chimed twelve, the first spirit appeared.

"Wake up, Ebeneezer. I am Ghost of Christmas Past. It is time for your first lesson."

Scrooge quickly realized he hadn't been dreaming! He looked around for a place to hide, but knew it was too late. If Marley was right, he had no choice.

With the spirit guiding him, they flew over the town and stopped by an old stone building. The spirit asked Scrooge if he knew where he was.

"Indeed, I do. That's my old school. And, that's me as a young man. I was so lonely then."

Scrooge had to stay at boarding school, while his friends went home for the holidays. "My father never missed a day of work. He used to say, 'Friends will desert you, but gold lasts forever!' Alas, it wasn't my friends who deserted me—it was my father!"

Passing through time, they stopped at the house of a beautiful young woman. The Ghost of Christmas Past pointed to the window. "Look, Ebeneezer, it's Elizabeth. You two were once engaged."

Elizabeth lay on her bed sobbing, "Ebeneezer loved his gold more than he loved me. Now, instead of a husband, I have a broken heart!"

Scrooge clutched his chest and said, "Poor Elizabeth! It hurts me to see her that way. I was so eager to build a fortune. I didn't take time for love. Why was I so blind?"

The minutes passed quickly and it was time to leave. The spirit led him home.

Wearily, Scrooge crawled into bed. The clock chimed once more, and the second spirit appeared. "I am the Ghost of Christmas Present. I will show you the way things are now."

"No! Leave me alone. I don't want to go."

But the Ghost of Christmas Present took Scrooge by the elbow and out through the window they flew.

They traveled swiftly through the city, until they came to Marian's house. "Oh, dear, she's crying, too! Why is she so sad?" asked Scrooge.

The spirit replied, "You're the only family she has, yet you wouldn't spend one day with her. Do you blame her, Scrooge?"

At the next house, they saw a small boy who was very sick. "That's your clerk's son, Tiny Tim. Cratchit can't afford Tim's medicine because you don't pay him enough."

"Will he ever get well?" asked Scrooge.

"Do you really care?"

"Yes! Even I hate to see a small child who's sick. Can Tim be helped?" he asked. The ghost was gone.

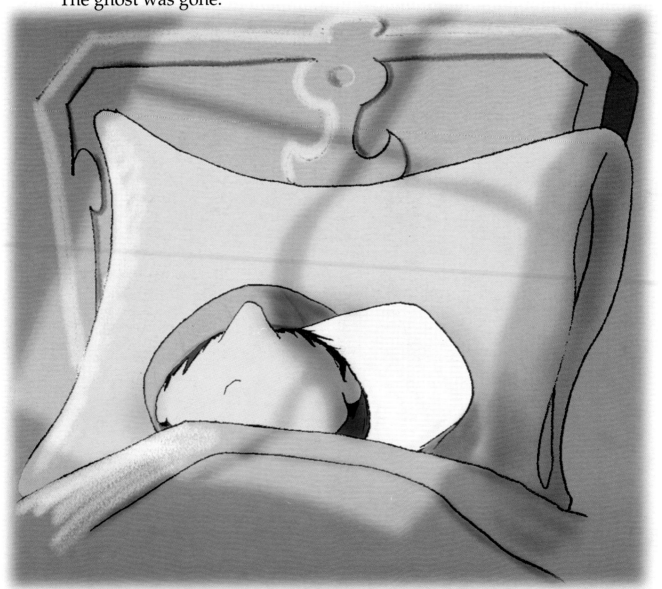

Scrooge wanted to rest, but the clock on the mantel wouldn't keep still.
At the sound of the chimes, the air turned icy.

A silent, solemn figure stood by the bed, draped in a hooded black shroud.

Frightened by this grim form, Scrooge shuddered. "You must be the Spirit of Christmas Yet to Come. Somehow, I fear this part most of all. Let's get it over with. I can't bear much more."

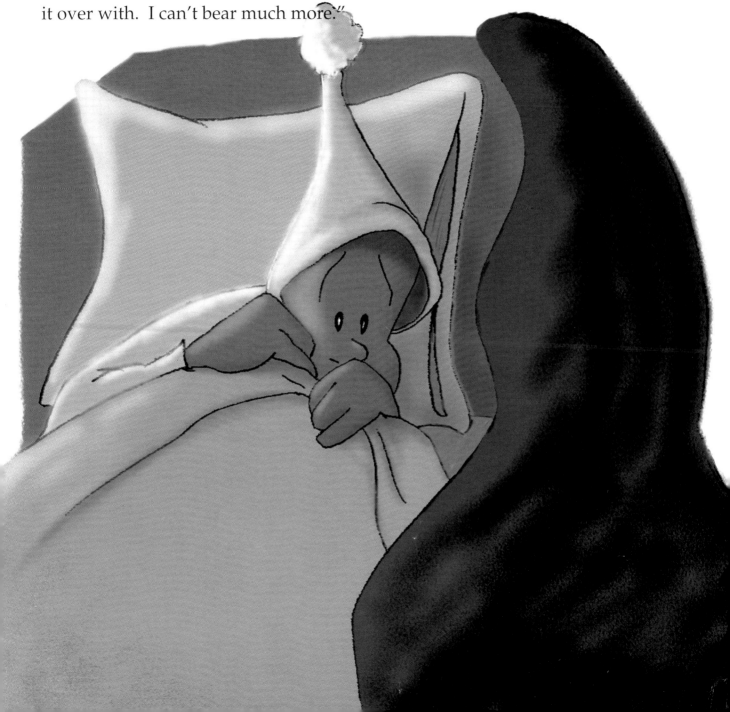

In the blink of an eye, Scrooge was at his shop. The windows were shuttered and the door boarded up. Marian was talking to Cratchit.

"He was my only relative, and never said anything kind to me."

Cratchit replied, "He was a cold-hearted man. He lived alone and died alone. No one will shed a tear tonight."

Scrooge tugged the ghost's sleeve. "Who are they talking about, Spirit? Is it me? Please - say it's not me!"

A damp fog filled the air. They were standing at the foot of a grave. The headstone read simply, *Ebeneezer Scrooge.*

"Show me no more! I was cruel and thoughtless—but not anymore. It's not too late for me. Is it, Spirit? Answer me, please," he begged.

There was no one there.

Wondering what tomorrow would bring, Scrooge fell into a restless sleep.

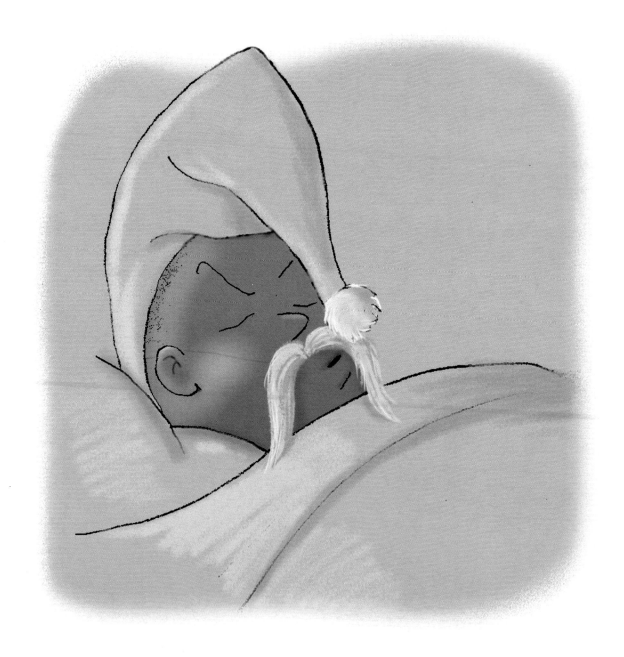

In the morning, the bright sun reflected off the newly fallen snow. Light patterns danced on the walls. Scrooge's first thought upon waking was: "I'm alive! Aah! What a glorious day."

He quickly got dressed thinking, "I hope the stores are still open. There's so much to do!"

Scrooge's first stop was the orphanage where he surprised Mr. Forbes with a whole bag of gold! Then, he went to Marian's house.

"Uncle Ebeneezer, what a nice surprise!"

"Get your coat, my dear, we're going visiting! First, we'll see if the butcher has a big, juicy turkey."

When Bob Cratchit opened the door that Christmas day, he had a surprise he never would forget.

There stood old man Scrooge, and Marian with a pile of gifts—and the biggest turkey anyone could imagine. Cratchit was speechless.

"Well? Aren't you going to invite us in," Scrooge asked.
Cratchit called to his family, "Look who came to visit!"

Mrs. Cratchit came out from the kitchen to greet their guests. "What a
lovely surprise. You've caught the spirit after all, Mr. Scrooge! Please sit down
and join us."

They took their places at the table and Cratchit let Scrooge carve the turkey.

"By the way, Bob, I'm giving you the rest of the week off—and a generous raise. After putting up with me all these years, you've earned it."

"Until now, I've thought only of myself and making money. How lucky I am to have seen the light in time to change my ways. It feels good to smile and be loved."

Everyone cheered and Marian hugged her uncle.

Tiny Tim was beaming. He'd never had a Christmas like this, ever. He reached up to hug Scrooge and said, "Merry Christmas, Mr. Scrooge. A very merry Christmas to us all!"

The End